W9-CFV-124

Barry's Best Buddy

Renée French

Barry's Best Buddy

A TOON BOOK BY

Renée French

TOON BOOKS IS AN IMPRINT OF CANDLEWICK PRESS

For Daphne

Editorial Director: FRANÇOISE MOULY

Book Design: FRANÇOISE MOULY & JONATHAN BENNETT

Guest Editors: NADJA SPIEGELMAN & LEIGH STEIN

Production: MYKEN BOMBERGER

RENÉE FRENCH'S artwork was drawn in pencil and colored digitally.

 Printed in Dongguan, Guangdong, China by Toppan Leefung.
Library of Congress Cataloging-in-Publication Data:
French, Renée.
Barry's best buddy : a TOON book / Renée French. p. cm.
Summary: Polarhog takes his reluctant best friend on a walk while a surprise is brewing. ISBN 978-1-935179-21-4
1. Graphic novels. [1. Graphic novels. 2. Best friends–Fiction. 3. Friendship–Fiction. 4. Surprise–Fiction.] I. Title.
PZ7.7.F78Bar 2013 741.5'973–dc23 2012022896

ISBN 13: 978-1-935179-21-4 ISBN 10: 1-935179-21-7

13 14 15 16 17 18 TPN 10 9 8 7 6 5 4 3 2 1

WWW.TOON-BOOKS.COM

Barry, **wake up**! It's me, Polarhog! I have a **SURPRISE** for you!
KNOCK KNOCK!

Polarhog! I was having a lovely **nap**!
Your **HOUSE** puts me to sleep. What **color** is it? **Snooze?**
It's **gray**.

Bor-ing!
Where is my surprise?
You'll see...

How do you do, ants?

Look! **Hats!**
I do **not** like hats.
NOT going to happen.
HATS

You'd look **SO good** in a hat.
Polarhog, I do ***not*** like hats.

This is the one for ***you***!
I do **NOT**...

...*like* hats.
How is this a good idea?

It makes you **look** like the king of **France**!
I **LOVE** my hat!
UMF!
UMF!

Polarhog, **what** do you want to **show** me?
Phew!
It's hot!
RED
BLUE

I'm so sweaty!

HEY! Where is your ***hat***?
Oh, ***tragedy***. I must have dropped it.

SNIFF!
I smell **ice cream**. Do you want any?
Ice cream has a **smell**?

I want a **blue** one!

One for **me** and one for ***my friend***!
ice cream
ICE CREA
No, thanks. I don't ***like*** ice cream.

Oh, happiness!
Oh, **BLISS**!

Tell me, **where** are we ***going***?
You'll see— it's not too far **now**.

Barry, have a **meatball**.
What? No thanks!

WAIT! ***Where*** did you get a ***meatball***?

Mmm...
I ***found*** it.
EW. Then ***maybe*** don't ***eat*** it.
Uh-oh.

Hey—we're **there**!
LOOK!
?!

Is that **my** house?
Yes, ***it is***!

But **HOW**...?
BARRY
The **ants**!

You did **this** for **ME**?
You're my **BEST FRIEND**.
SNIFF! It's ***beautiful***!
Y

BARRY
Ta-da!
Happy birthday!
We love to decorate!
R
R

Oh, **good**—
you found my
hat!
BARRY
R
R

Thanks, Polarhog, I **LOVE** the house.
Anytime!
Hey, would you like **my** hat?
You know what? **No thanks.**

ABOUT THE AUTHOR

RENÉE FRENCH lives in California with her husband Rob in a beige-colored house. The best birthday present she got as a child was a giant box of art supplies as big as her body. Growing up, she would play hooky from school in order to lie on the couch all day and draw—which, in fact, is exactly what she does all day long now. Renowned as the author of many books of comics for both adults and children (including *H Day*, *Micrographia*, and *The Ticking*), she's been nominated for best artist by the Eisner, Harvey, and Ignatz Awards. Like Polarhog, she has always loved blue Popsicles. The ants in this book are inspired by ants in her own neighborhood, who she's certain must be busy decorating something, somewhere.

TIPS FOR PARENTS AND TEACHERS:

HOW TO READ COMICS WITH KIDS

Kids love comics! They are naturally drawn to the details in the pictures, which make them want to read the words. Comics beg for repeated readings and let both emerging and reluctant readers enjoy complex stories with a rich vocabulary. But since comics have their own grammar, here are a few tips for reading them with kids:

GUIDE YOUNG READERS: Use your finger to show your place in the text, but keep it at the bottom of the speaking character so it doesn't hide the very important facial expressions.

HAM IT UP! Think of the comic book story as a play and don't hesitate to read with expression and intonation. Assign parts or get kids to supply the sound effects, a great way to reinforce phonics skills.

LET THEM GUESS. Comics provide lots of context for the words, so emerging readers can make informed guesses. Like jigsaw puzzles, comics ask readers to make connections, so check a young audience's understanding by asking "What's this character thinking?" (but don't be surprised if a kid finds some of the comics' subtle details faster than you).

TALK ABOUT THE PICTURES. Point out how the artist paces the story with pauses (silent panels) or speeded-up action (a burst of short panels). Discuss how the size and shape of the panels carry meaning.

ABOVE ALL, ENJOY! There is, of course, never one right way to read, so go for the shared pleasure. Once children make the story happen in their imaginations, they have discovered the thrill of reading, and you won't be able to stop them. At that point, just go get them more books, and more comics.